A DREAMER'S HEART
An Island Song

For Marie and Pat —
Dreams are what make you the good friends you are!
with love and gentle thoughts,
Frances Scarcille
November 1999

By Frances Scarcille

FOXGLOVE

P·R·E·S·S

Paintings by Freiman Stoltzfus

A DREAMER'S HEART
An Island Song

By Frances Scarcille
Paintings by Freiman Stoltzfus

Book design by Frances Scarcille and Freiman Stoltzfus
© Copyright 1997 by Frances Scarcille and Freiman Stoltzfus
Third printing, 1999.

FOXGLOVE

Foxglove Press
PO Box 1127
Bryn Mawr, PA 19010

P·R·E·S·S

ISBN 0-9659008-2-7
Library of Congress Catalogue #97-090692

Summary: With a simple and lilting text, this "island song" is
about dreams and what really matters in life. A timeless gift book
for all ages.

Printed in the USA
by the Mack Printing Group

To my parents; and to my godson, Max.

– Frances –

To my sister, Grace.

– Freiman –

This book is for children of all ages . . .

. . . for anyone who understands.

One beautiful starry night, on a faraway island
many miles out at sea, a little girl knelt to say
her prayers.

When she had finished giving thanks for all her blessings, she climbed into her big cozy bed beside the open window.

And looking up at the brightest star in the sky, she said,

"I wish I were
   As pretty as a princess,
   As rich as a king,
   As special as a flower
   On the first day of Spring."

She was a dreamer, as little girls often are
at that age.

When the little girl grew to be a teenager, she would walk home from the library on crisp Fall evenings. She would hear the leaves crackle beneath her feet.

And looking up at the brightest star in the sky, she would say,

"I wish I were
As pretty as a princess,
As rich as a king,
As special as a flower
On the first day of Spring."

She had been told not to be such a dreamer, but she was bored and restless, as girls often are at that age.

When the young girl grew up to be a woman, she married and had a little son. She became very busy taking care of her family.

She forgot all about her own dreams,
as women often do at that age.

One day her little boy came home from school with an essay he had written called "My Favorite Person". As she read his words, happy tears filled her eyes, because it was about *her* that he had written . . . how wonderful he thought she was—and how pretty.

She realized that the little wish she had long ago forgotten had been granted.

That night the woman went in to give her
sleeping boy a kiss. As she passed his open
window, she looked up at the brightest star
in the sky and said to herself,

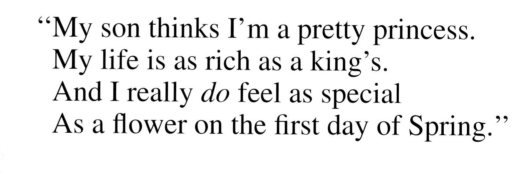

"My son thinks I'm a pretty princess.
My life is as rich as a king's.
And I really *do* feel as special
As a flower on the first day of Spring."

Many years later when she was an old, old woman, she would sit on her porch watching the ocean waves in the moonlight.

And looking up at the brightest star in the sky, she felt peaceful. She smiled.

The tapestry of her being had been woven
with fibers of kindness and compassion and honor.

And she encouraged others to dream,
as people often do at that age.

One day the angels called her to them.
Those who had been a part of her life
came together and carved a stone to remember her.

On the stone, these words were chiseled:

"Her *heart* made her a pretty princess.
  She was as special as a flower in Spring,
  And anyone who knew her is richer than a king."